Ann Turnbull

I was born in 1943 and grew up in Bexleyheath in South East London.

I have always loved books. My childhood favourites were the Narnia books by C S Lewis and Kipling's Jungle Books.

I started writing at a very early age and by the time I was ten had decided I wanted to be a writer. My first book was *The Frightened Forest*, which was published in 1974.

I live in Telford, Shropshire, with my husband Tim and our two children, David and Julie. We have a black cat called Sukey.

British Library Cataloguing in Publication Data
Turnbull, Ann
  Never a witch's cat
  I. Title   II. Morris, Tony *(date)*
  823'.914[J]
  ISBN 0-7214-1197-5

First edition

Published by Ladybird Books Ltd Loughborough Leicestershire UK
Ladybird Books Inc Auburn Maine 04210 USA
Paperbird is an imprint of Ladybird Books Ltd
© Text ANN TURNBULL MCMLXXXIX
© LADYBIRD BOOKS LTD MCMLXXXIX
Printed in England

Never a witch's cat

by ANN TURNBULL
illustrated by TONY MORRIS

Paperbird

Tabitha's warning

The Hallowe'en moon was huge and bright. It rose above the rooftops like a face and stared in through the window of Mrs May's Home for Stray Cats.

Willow, the grey cat, sat on the windowsill. The other cats slept by the fire. They began to stir and stretch as the moonlight woke them.

Ginger stood up and arched his back. Bella yawned. Lucky jumped out of the knitting basket. Only old Tabitha stayed curled in a knot by the fire.

Ginger ran to the cat flap and pushed it open.

The cold air woke Tabitha. "Ginger!" she said. "Don't go out tonight!"

"Why not?" asked Ginger.

"Why not?" asked all the others.

"It's Hallowe'en," said Tabitha. "The Witch will be about, looking for new servants. Do you want to be a witch's cat?"

"No!" they said.

But they loved the moonlight; they wanted to go outside.

"She keeps them in a cold castle," said Tabitha. "She feeds them on scraps. And she changes their eyes. You can always tell a witch's cat by its eyes. Do you want to be like them?"

"No!"

But the night air blew in, and they loved to hunt at night. And as for the Witch – perhaps that was just one of Tabitha's stories.

"How do you know?" asked Bella.

"Once in a while," said Tabitha, "not often, but once in a while, a cat escapes. My great-great-great-grandmother was one of those cats."

"That was a long time ago," said Ginger. He wanted to pounce and spring and howl at the moon.

Bella, the black cat, looked out of the window longingly. She wanted to feel the night wind in her fur.

Lucky miaowed, "Help! The Witch is after me!" He thought it was a joke.

Ginger made up his mind. He went out through the cat flap. Bella followed him, with Lucky close behind.

Only Willow hesitated. She was a nervous cat. The people who had owned her before she'd come to Mrs May's had treated her cruelly.

"Don't go out, Willow," said Tabitha. "Come and sit by the fire."

But Willow was on the windowsill, looking out at the dark.

Dry leaves blew past, crackling. She wanted to chase them. She leapt down from the sill, ran to the cat flap, and jumped out into the night.

The Witch

Willow ran down the street. She was going to the Singing Place.

The singing had already begun when she arrived. Ginger and Lucky sat wailing on the broken wall. Bella was with them. Her tail was fluffed up, her eyes like two gold moons. Willow crept into the shadows beneath the dustbins. She wanted to hear the singing, but she was nervous; she remembered Tabitha's warning.

The singing grew louder. Ginger howled. Lucky wailed.

A shadow crossed the moon.

Willow cried out, "The Witch! The Witch is coming!"

But they didn't hear her.

A dark shape, blacker than the night, rose up, filling the sky, and far up in the stars Willow saw the huge face of the Witch.

The Witch laughed. Her laughter was louder than the cats' song. Bella, Ginger and Lucky leapt from the wall, and Willow ran out from her hiding place. But the Witch was faster than all of them.

Two long arms reached out of t[...] throwing something down. The ca[...] caught – shut in the dark. They s[...] from side to side, but there was no way out. They were in the Witch's bag.

"Ginger? Are you there?" asked Bella.

"Yes."

"And Lucky?"

"Yes."

"And me, too," said Willow.

The bag rose off the ground. It was flying through the air, gathering speed. The cats began to miaow.

"I want to go home!" cried Lucky.

"Let us out! Let us out!" cried Bella and Willow.

At last they felt a bump. They were back on the ground. They stopped miaowing, but from outside the bag came other sounds: hissing and snarling. The bag was being prodded, and they felt claws poking through.

Ginger's fur bristled. He sank his teeth into the bag, tore a hole, and burst out, hissing.

Outside were a gang of about a dozen cats – the most wicked-looking cats he had ever seen. They were thin and scruffy, with scarred faces and bitten ears, and they all had strange, glittering eyes.

The cats laughed at Ginger.

"Oh! Isn't he brave! A fighter, is he? We'll soon sort him out!"

But when Ginger arched his back and fluffed up his fur and glared at them they all drew back a step.

Bella and Lucky were out of the bag now, with Willow hiding behind them. The Witch's cats saw them. They made fun of Bella.

"Here's a pretty one! Look at her long black whiskers! Look at her fluffy tail! She won't be so pretty when she's starved and dirty and covered in fleas!"

The Witch's cats picked Lucky up and tossed him around like a football. Willow, hiding at the back, hoped she would not be noticed, but they pulled her out and scratched and hissed at her.

"Skinny little thing! Not worth the bother. Should have left her behind."

"Don't hurt her!" said Bella, who was licking Lucky's scratches. "Tell us what's going to happen to us. Where are we? And where is the Witch?"

At the mention of the word *Witch*, the scruffy cats all fell flat on the floor and grovelled.

The four friends looked around. The room they were in had a stone floor and stone walls. Grey nets of cobweb hung from the ceiling. Bones lay on the floor. At the far end of the room was a doorway with stairs going up from it. In the doorway hung a fur curtain. Willow saw that the fur was a patchwork of tabby, grey, ginger, white and black. A row of cats' tails hung from the edge. She stared at it in horror.

The Witch's cats had stopped grovelling. A tabby who seemed to be their leader grinned wickedly and said, "I see you like our curtain. Pretty, isn't it? Cats don't last long in this job. That's why You-Know-Who needs more cats every Hallowe'en."

"But – what do you have to do?" asked Bella.

The cats showed her. One of them pretended to catch a mouse; another pretended to chase flies.

"We catch things," said the leader. "Mice, and rats, and spiders, and bats, and cockroaches, and flies, and toads, and slugs, and birds, and woodlice, and moths...

You-Know-Who needs all sorts of
ingredients for her spells; she's always
stirring things in that cauldron up there."
He turned his head towards the ceiling.

One of the cats fell flat on its back with
its paws in the air. The others laughed.

"Oh, yes." The leader grinned. "And
cats. She often has cats, or parts of cats,
on her list of ingredients."

The cats rolled about laughing.

"But don't you care?" cried Bella. "Haven't you tried to escape?"

The cats all looked at Bella out of their strange eyes.

"Wait till your eyes are like ours," they said. "Then you'll be one of us."

"You'll see," said a white one.

"Soon," said a black one.

Bella was frightened. "How soon?"

"As soon as You-Know-Who comes through that curtain," said the leader.

The four friends looked at each other.

"There must be a way out," said Ginger.

"There is," the leader said. "It's quick – but rather smelly."

He led them to a windowsill. In it was a hole, and from this hole came a dreadful smell. They sprang back, choking. The Witch's cats laughed. Ginger looked in again. He saw that the hole was a chute which led down to a place outside the castle wall.

"Where does it come out?" asked Ginger.

"In the ditch!" shrieked the laughing cats.

"Is it full of water?"

"No! Just rubbish – and dead cats."

Willow shuddered. But Bella said, "What do we do if we get out of the ditch?"

"Follow the path," laughed the cats. "Just follow the path until you reach the wall!"

There was a sound of footsteps overhead. All the cats stopped talking.

The footsteps crossed the room and the four friends heard them coming down the stairs towards the fur curtain.

"Quick!" said Bella. "Down the chute! It's our only chance."

Willow said, "I can't... I daren't..."

The footsteps stopped.

A hand seized the fur curtain.

The Witch's cats fell flat on the floor and grovelled.

"Now!" cried Ginger. He sprang onto the windowsill and leapt down the chute. Lucky followed him.

Willow clung to the edge.

"Jump, Willow! Jump!" cried Bella.

The fur curtain was flung aside, and the Witch in her black cloak flowed into the room.

"My new arrivals!" she hissed. "Let me see their eyes!"

"No!" cried Willow and Bella together.

They shut their eyes and jumped.

Spells

They landed in a ditch. It was full to the brim with bones, tins, dead rats and dead cats.

They tried to go quietly across it, but as they climbed up the far bank, Lucky trod on a tin that fell tinkling onto the bones below. The sound was loud in the silence. They froze.

Nothing moved. There was no sound from the castle.

"Perhaps we've beaten her," whispered Bella. "Perhaps we are free now."

"I don't think so," said Willow.

And yet the way looked clear. The moon lit the path, and only a short way ahead the wall was shining white against the dark sky. "Follow the path until you reach the wall," the Witch's cats had said.

They padded along the path: Ginger in the lead, then Bella, then Lucky and Willow.

It was Lucky who stopped first. He sat down and said, "I'm tired. Are we nearly there?"

They all stopped and looked ahead. The wall was further away than it had been when they were back at the ditch. They stared, unbelieving.

"We've come the wrong way," said Ginger.

"No," said Bella. "The wall is still there. It just wasn't as near as we thought."

They went on. But the wall, instead of growing nearer, began to seem further away than ever. Before long it had disappeared. Tall trees shut out the sky, bushes grew around them, and they could not see the path.

"We *must* have come the wrong way," said Ginger.

"It's the Witch," said Willow. "We haven't escaped her. This is one of her spells."

They crept along. The trees crowded closer together, hiding the moon. The four cats felt as if they were walking in circles.

At last they saw that there was more light, and – their hearts leapt – the wall, only a few yards away.

"We've won!" cried Lucky.

He sprang out and ran along the path.

A shadow moved between him and the stars.

The cats looked up.

The Witch was riding on her broomstick above the trees.

She saw Lucky and turned the broomstick down towards him. Lucky tried to run away. The Witch shrieked with laughter. She shot over his head and blocked his way. He turned back to the path, but she blocked his way again. He ran first one way, then another, but whichever way he turned the Witch was faster.

Lucky grew angry. He hissed and struck up at her with his claws. The Witch laughed, and rose out of reach.

As she flew away they saw her pull out a small bag. She threw it down. The bag split above Lucky's head and grey powder drifted over him. He sneezed and a bright light flashed.

"Croak!" said Lucky.

The others crept out of the wood and stared at him in horror. He had turned into a toad.

"Croak?" asked Lucky. He felt strange, and wondered why his friends looked so upset.

The house in the marsh

For a long time the four friends hid in the wood. Willow and Bella wanted to give up, but Ginger urged them on. They set off again, and Lucky followed behind them: hop, hop, hop.

Once again the road began to grow longer, and the wall seemed far away. They came to a marsh. The path was flooded and the cats hated water. Even Ginger began to despair, but he tried not to show it.

"We must go on," he said.

Bella would not listen to him. "Lucky is under a spell. What's the use of escaping now Lucky is a toad?"

"I'm sure that if we can reach the wall the spell will wear off," said Ginger. "The Witch has no power outside the wall."

"But we can't reach the wall!" wailed Bella.

"It gets further and further away!" cried Willow.

"We've got to try," said Ginger. "If we give up, the Witch has won. Other cats have escaped. Tabitha told us. Remember?"

"I remember," said Willow. "Let's try."

The path led on and on across the marsh. Lightning flashed, and it began to rain. The cats scuttled along the path, tails down, ears flat, with soaking fur. Only Lucky enjoyed it. He hopped along happily, *plop, squelch, plop, squelch,* wondering why water had never seemed such fun before.

Lucky was leading the way. Willow, running blindly in the rain behind him, heard *plop, squelch, splash!* and opened her eyes wide. The marsh had become a lake. Lucky was swimming. Bella and Willow miaowed miserably.

"Look!" said Ginger.

They looked. On the far side of the lake was the wall: white, solid, real, and nearer than it had ever been before.

"If we can swim across the lake we've beaten her," said Ginger. He plunged into the water. Willow urged Bella forward. They both cried out at the cold water, but they swam, following Ginger and Lucky. At last they crawled out onto the path on the far side.

And there all was changed. The wall was gone, but in its place was their own familiar street with its houses and railings and walls and gardens; and there, right in front of them, was Mrs May's Home for Stray Cats. The door was open, and Mrs May herself stood in the doorway, smiling and calling them in.

"We've done it!" cried Ginger. "We're home!"

He marched ahead of them up the path towards Mrs May. He went in through the doorway.

"No! Wait!" cried Willow. Something was wrong. It was too easy. They hadn't crossed the wall. And Lucky was still a toad. "Wait!" she pleaded.

Too late. As Ginger stepped over the threshold, Willow saw the figure of Mrs May change and grow. The small nose grew long and hooked and reached down to meet the chin. The green knitted cardigan turned black and wide and billowing; it wrapped around Ginger as he rubbed against her legs.

The door slammed shut. Willow heard cackling laughter and saw the Witch shoot up and out through the chimney. Laughing triumphantly, the Witch flew round the house on her broomstick before flying away across the marsh.

Willow looked down. The familiar street was gone. The marsh spread all around. Only the house was still there. And it was not Mrs May's house at all. It never had been. How could she have thought it was?

And then she saw Ginger – or all that could be seen of him. Ginger was inside the house, but his tail was outside, shut fast in the door, and he was howling in pain and fear.

Magic words

Willow and Bella jumped up and pressed on the door with their front paws. It would not move. They scrabbled at the base. They tried to slip a paw into a crack, but there was no crack wide enough. Ginger's tail was stuck.

"It's a spell!" sobbed Bella.

Willow sat next to her and licked her head. She was usually too nervous to lick other cats – especially Bella, who had always seemed so clever, so big, bossy and beautiful. But now Bella was not bossy at all; she needed Willow to comfort her.

"Magic words undo spells," said Willow. "I'll try some."

She turned to the door.

"Abracadabra?" she tried. "Open Sesame?"

The door stayed shut.

She tried politeness. "Door, please open and let Ginger go."

The door stayed shut.

She tried firmness. "Door! Open!"

The door stayed shut.

"It's no good," wept Bella. "We'll never guess the words."

"You're right," said Willow. "There's only one place to find out what the magic words are. I'll have to go back to the Witch's castle."

"Go back?" cried Bella. "But she'll turn you into a witch's cat. She'll change your eyes –"

"Not if I'm careful," said Willow.

"Don't go!" begged Bella. "Don't leave me."

"I'll soon come back."

"But I'll be all alone!"

"You've got Lucky – in a way. And Ginger. At least, you've got his tail."

"How will you find the castle?" asked
Bella. "The Witch changes everything.
We never found the wall."

"I think it will be easier going back,"
said Willow.

And she was right.

As soon as she turned round and began
padding back along the path, the rain
stopped, the marsh dried up, and in no
time at all she was standing outside the
great door of the castle. On the door was a
cat flap shaped like a cat's face. The face
grinned and said, "Welcome home!"

Willow to the rescue

Willow had a plan. It was a desperate plan. She knew she would have to be brave to carry it out.

She pushed through the grinning cat flap, and heard it lock behind her.

The Witch's cats were waiting. They pounced on her, pushing and scratching.

"Leave me alone!" said Willow. "Listen to me. I can help you all to escape."

The cats laughed. "What for? Didn't do you much good, did it? Wait till You-Know-Who gets back. It'll be the flea pit for you!"

"The others have almost reached the wall," said Willow.

"Almost at the wall?" the leader said. "That's not what You-Know-Who told us. *She* says the black and white one has been turned into a toad and the big ginger one has got his tail stuck in a door. It's a strong spell, that one. And you don't know the words to free him."

The cats laughed. One cat hopped round the room croaking and another pretended to be Ginger, pulling on his trapped tail and miaowing.

Willow sighed. She knew she would never persuade them. They were the Witch's slaves. They could not help being stupid and cruel. Yet she was determined to rescue them all if she could.

She turned an ear towards the ceiling, but heard nothing. The Witch must be away. It was time for her plan.

She edged closer to the rubbish chute.

"What special words will free Ginger?" she asked.

They laughed. "Think we'd tell you?"

"You don't know the words," said
Willow.

"Yes, we do!" The cats were indignant.

"Tell me, then," said Willow.

"No!"

"I don't believe you know them," said
Willow. "You-Know-Who wouldn't tell
you. You're slaves. You don't count for
anything."

She was moving closer to the chute. The
cats were angry now. They hissed and put
out their claws. Another moment and they
would jump on her.

"You're so low," said Willow, "that I've only got to say the word *Witch* and you all fall flat and grovel."

By the time Willow said *grovel*, all the cats were grovelling.

The one who recovered first – a little one – shouted, "*I'm* not a slave! *I* know! It's:

> Magic words
> Make a key –"

"Be quiet!" shouted the others. "She'll beat us! She'll starve us! She'll drop us in the flea pit!"

"He can't remember any more," said Willow. She was very near the chute.

"I can!" he shouted.
> "Magic words
> Make a key;
> Door unlock,
> Tail go free –"

The other cats tried to stop him, but he fought them off.

"Free go tail" – he gasped –
"Unlock door – I *do* know it! Get off!"

Larger cats sat on him and muffled him, but Willow's keen ears caught his last words:
> "Free as whisker,
> Free as paw."

Willow jumped onto the windowsill.

"Stop her!" yelled the leader. "She's away!"

The mob turned on Willow. Willow took a deep breath and, in the biggest voice she had ever produced, she cried, "WITCH!"

The Witch's cats fell flat on the floor and grovelled.

Willow leapt down the chute.

Race to freedom

In the ditch, Willow waited, just long enough to be sure that her plan was working.

It was. She heard the leader screech, "Down the chute! All of you! Don't let her escape! She's got the words! You-Know-Who will kill us for this!"

As the first witch's cat shot down the chute Willow sprang across the ditch, leapt up the far side and was away, racing along the path. The words of the spell were in her mind:

> "Magic words
> Make a key;
> Door unlock,
> Tail go free.
> Free go tail,
> Unlock door,
> Free as whisker,
> Free as paw."

And again:

> "Magic words
> Make a key..."

Over and over again she said them to
herself. She knew she must not get them
wrong when she reached the house. There
would not be time for mistakes.

The way was clear: no woods, no storm,
no marsh; only the path leading on, and
the wall in the distance.

Once she looked back. The Witch's cats
were racing along behind her. If they
caught her, they would tear her to pieces.
Fear gave her strength she did not know
she had. She ran so fast that she scarcely
felt herself move; it was like flying. And
the words – the words that would save
Ginger – beat their rhythm in her head:

> "Magic words
>   Make a key;
>   Door unlock,
>   Tail go free…"

"Catch her! Kill her!" the Witch's cats
cried.

But they were thin and under-fed. Willow was slim and strong and filled with power. The Witch's cats began to quarrel amongst themselves as they ran: "It's all your fault!" "You told her!" "You let her escape!" "Who grovelled first, then?"

Their leader hissed at them, "Catch her! Kill her!" He drove them on.

Willow was winning. The path flew by under her paws. Nothing could stop her. The gap between her and the Witch's cats grew. Ahead of her on the path she saw the house, and behind it the wall, real and solid as the wall of the Singing Place. She was there. She would save them all.

She reached the door of the house: Ginger's tail stuck out, Lucky croaked, Bella miaowed. Willow gasped, "Bella! I've got the words!"

She took a deep breath. Behind her she felt a shadow, a cold air rising. The Witch! Firmly Willow spoke:

"Magic words
Make a key;
Door unlock,
Tail go free.
Free go tail,
Unlock door,
Free as whisker,
Free as paw."

For a moment nothing happened. Willow felt her heart thudding. Then there was a flash of light, a cry from Ginger, and the door swung open. Ginger walked free. First to greet him was Lucky, rubbing against him and purring.

"Lucky!" cried Bella. "You're back!"

From the sky came a scream of rage. The Witch was flying towards them on her broomstick. And now Bella, her eyes black with fear, cried, "Look!"

The Witch's cats were coming, racing along the path, all teeth and claws and cruel eyes. "Catch her! Kill her!" they cried.

"The wall!" said Ginger.

The wall. Behind the house it rose: high, white and sheer. No one knew what was on the other side. Perhaps the Witch's cats had lied. Perhaps it was a trap. But they had no choice.

"Quickly," said Willow. "Up. Up and over."

They jumped: Bella, Lucky, Ginger. Up and over. Then Willow – and behind her, just as she had planned, the Witch's cats, unable to stop: up and over the wall.

And as the last one leapt to freedom the Witch screamed her fury in the sky above.

Home

Willow felt a bump, and opened her eyes.

She was on the wall of the Singing Place. Ginger, Bella and Lucky sat beside her.

"I had a strange feeling," said Bella, "as if I had floated down from a great height."

"So did I," said Willow. She had fallen slowly, legs out, like a flying squirrel.

"A dandelion seed," said Lucky. "That's what I felt like."

Willow wondered if she had been dreaming.

"Do you remember..." she began.

"The Witch," said Bella.

"The castle," said Ginger.

"The cats," said Lucky.

They all began to talk at once.

"Willow," said Ginger, "you saved us."

"No," said Willow. "We did it together. You made us go on when we wanted to give up."

"And Bella looked after me when I was... not myself," said Lucky. "What *did* happen to me?"

"You turned into a toad," they said.

"Don't be silly," said Lucky.

"Home," said Bella, purring. "We can go home now."

They noticed then that all around them, on the wall, on the dustbins, and on the ground, were other cats. They looked a little like the cats from the Witch's castle, but these cats were fatter, fluffier, friendlier. And their eyes were quite different.

The moon was fading in the pale sky. It was time to go. Cats sprang lightly down from wall and dustbin and padded off along empty streets.

High up in the sky above the Singing Place the Witch was shrinking. She shrank and shrank until she was no bigger than a dot. Soon there was nothing left of her at all.

As the sun rose, large numbers of cats arrived at Mrs May's Home for Stray Cats. Cats were everywhere: on chairs, on windowsills, in baskets and boxes, miaowing around chair legs, purring as they lapped milk.

Willow and Tabitha sat close together by the fire.

Tabitha said, "The Witch will not come back. Her power has been broken. It must have begun to weaken as soon as you went back to the castle to rescue all the cats."

"So that's why she never caught me on my way to free Ginger?"

"Yes. Her power could only be broken by a cat who was brave enough to risk her own life for the others. When you all escaped together, that was the end of the Witch's power."

Willow was thoughtful. "I didn't know I could be brave," she said.

Mrs May came and set down a saucer of milk on the hearth. She stroked Willow's head. Once Willow would have shrunk away, but now she pressed up against the hand and purred.

The milk was warm. Willow and Tabitha bent their heads to the saucer and lapped contentedly.

PAPERBIRD

If you have enjoyed this story look out for other PAPERBIRD titles:

Night school
by ROBERT SWINDELLS

Why are things often moved or missing from the classroom? Why do the cleaners clean the school twice? Lucy and Jen decide to return to school one evening to find out who or WHAT uses their school at night...

Stone of mystery
by BETTE MEYRICK

Yvonne is given a pendant of stone mined from the same Welsh hillside which provided the stone for Stonehenge. But it seems that someone from the past desperately wants the piece of stone in the pendant returned...

Phantom from the past
by SUSAN PRICE

When the school decides to have a Victorian day as part of their history lesson, all the children and teachers dress in Victorian costume to re-enact a school day in the nineteenth century. But as the lesson wears on, one of the teachers seems to be taking things very seriously and she no longer seems to be acting...

Candy stops a train
Candy goes to the gymkhana
both by CHRISTINE PULLEIN-THOMPSON

Two books about Neil, Liz and Vicky Fraser and their pony, Candy.

In **Candy stops a train** they discover that the pony is missing. The Frasers find themselves in a desperate race against time to get Candy back before there is a terrible accident.

In **Candy goes to the gymkhana** the children enter Candy in several events. After weeks of preparation the day of the gymkhana arrives and everyone is hopeful of winning lots of rosettes. But it begins to look as though they won't win anything.